Anna and the Dance Class

The Sound of Short A

by Cecilia Minden and Joanne Meier • illustrated by Bob Ostrom

Published by The Child's World®
1980 Lookout Drive
Mankato, MN 56003-1705
800-599-READ
www.childsworld.com

The Child's World®: Mary Berendes, Publishing Director
The Design Lab: Design and page production

Library of Congress Cataloging-in-Publication Data
Minden, Cecilia.
  Anna and the dance class : the sound of short A /
by Cecilia Minden and Joanne Meier ; illustrated
by Bob Ostrom.
    p. cm.
  ISBN 978-1-60253-392-9 (library bound : alk. paper)
  1. English language—Vowels—Juvenile literature.
  2. English language—Phonetics—Juvenile literature.
  3. Reading—Phonetic method—Juvenile literature.
  I. Meier, Joanne D. II. Ostrom, Bob. III. Title.
  PE1157.M5633 2010
  [E]—dc22
                                    2010005616

Printed in the United States of America in Mankato, MN.
July 2010
F11538

NOTE TO PARENTS AND EDUCATORS:

The Child's World® has created this series with the goal of exposing children to engaging stories and illustrations that assist in phonics development. The books in the series will help children learn the relationships between the letters of written language and the individual sounds of spoken language. This contact helps children learn to use these relationships to read and write words.

The books in this series follow a similar format. An introductory page, to be read by an adult, introduces the child to the phonics feature, or sound, that will be highlighted in the book. Read this page to the child, stressing the phonic feature. Help the student learn how to form the sound with her mouth. The story and engaging illustrations follow the introduction. At the end of the story, word lists categorize the feature words into their phonic elements.

Each book in this series has been carefully written to meet specific readability requirements. Close attention has been paid to elements such as word count, sentence length, and vocabulary. Readability formulas measure the ease with which the text can be read and understood. Each book in this series has been analyzed using the Spache readability formula.

Reading research suggests that systematic phonics instruction can greatly improve students' word recognition, spelling, and comprehension skills. This series assists in the teaching of phonics by providing students with important opportunities to apply their knowledge of phonics as they read words, sentences, and text.

The letter a makes two sounds.

The long sound of **a** sounds like **a** as in: *cake* and *date*.

The short sound of **a** sounds like **a** as in: *cat* and *add*.

In this book, you will read words that have the short **a** sound as in: *dance, bag, apple,* and *tap.*

Anna likes to dance.

Her shoes are in her bag.

Anna has an apple in her bag. The apple is for her teacher, Miss Alice.

Anna gives Miss Alice the apple.

"Thank you, Anna," says Miss Alice.

Anna puts on her tap shoes.

She gets in the line.

Miss Alice claps her hands.

The music begins.

Miss Alice taps her foot.

Anna taps her foot.

The girls clap and tap.

They tap around the room.

Anna likes to hear her tapping toes!

Anna loves to dance!

It makes her happy.

Fun Facts

Not all apples are red—some are green or yellow, too. There are 7,500 different types of apples grown all over the world. Some apple trees can live for more than 100 years! The states that produce the most apples are Washington, New York, Michigan, California, Pennsylvania, and Virginia. In Michigan, the blossom found on apple trees is the state flower.

Tap dancing is a combination of English, Scottish, Irish, and African cultures. Metal is attached to the heels and toes of tap shoes. This is what makes the tapping noise when dancers perform. Before metal was used, some tap dancers used shoes made of wood. Tap dancing became popular in the United States in the late 1800s.

Activity

Apple Picking

If you like apples, then you should consider going apple picking with your family. Certain farms and orchards allow people to collect apples and then take them home. Apple picking usually begins in the fall. When you get home, you and your parents can bake an apple pie for the whole family to enjoy!

To Learn More

Books
About the Sound of Short A
Moncure, Jane Belk. *My "a" Sound Box®*. Mankato, MN: The Child's World, 2009.

About Apples
Maestro, Betsy, and Giulio Maestro (illustrator). *How Do Apples Grow?* New York: HarperCollins, 1992.

Ziefert, Harriet, and Karla Gudeon (illustrator). *One Red Apple*. Maplewood, NJ: Blue Apple Books, 2009.

About Clapping Hands
Bernstein, Sara. *Hand Clap! "Miss Mary Mack" and 42 Other Handclapping Games for Children*. Holbrook, MA: Adams Media Corporation, 1994.

Cauley, Lorinda Bryan. *Clap Your Hands*. Orlando, FL: Harcourt Brace, 1992.

About Tap Dancing
Brisson, Pat, and Nancy Cote (illustrator). *Tap-dance Fever*. Honesdale, PA: Boyds Mills Press, 2005.

Dillon, Leo, and Diane Dillon. *Rap A Tap Tap*. New York: Blue Sky Press, 2002.

Web Sites
Visit our home page for lots of links about the Sound of Short A:

childsworld.com/links

Note to Parents, Teachers, and Librarians: We routinely check our Web links to make sure they're safe, active sites—so encourage your readers to check them out!

Short A
Feature Words

Proper Names
Alice
Anna

Feature Words in Initial Position
apple

Feature Words in Medial Position
bag
clap
dance
hand
happy
tap
tapping

About the Authors

Cecilia Minden, PhD, is the former director of the Language and Literacy Program at the Harvard Graduate School of Education. She is now a reading consultant for school and library publications. She earned her PhD in reading education from the University of Virginia. Cecilia and her husband, Dave Cupp, live outside Chapel Hill, North Carolina. They enjoy sharing their love of reading with their grandchildren, Chelsea and Qadir.

Joanne Meier, PhD, has worked as an elementary school teacher, university professor, and researcher. She earned her BA in early childhood education from the University of South Carolina, and her MEd and PhD in education from the University of Virginia. She currently works as a literacy consultant for schools and private organizations. Joanne lives in Virginia with her husband Eric, daughters Kella and Erin, two cats, and a gerbil.

About the Illustrator

Bob Ostrom has been illustrating children's books for nearly twenty years. A graduate of the New England School of Art & Design at Suffolk University, Bob has worked for such companies as Disney, Nickelodeon, and Cartoon Network. He lives in North Carolina with his wife Melissa and three children, Will, Charlie, and Mae.